Rebecca Emberley and Ed Emberley

Ten Little Beasties

A Neal Porter Book
Roaring Brook Press
New York

Copyright © 2011 by Rebecca Emberley Inc.
A Neal Porter Book
Published by Roaring Brook Press
Roaring Brook Press is a division of Holtzbrinck Publishing Holdings Limited Partnership
175 Fifth Avenue, New York, New York 10010
mackids.com

Library of Congress Cataloging-in-Publication Data
Emberley, Rebecca.
Ten little beasties / Rebecca Emberley and Ed Emberley.
   p.   cm.
"A Neal Porter book."
Summary: One by one, ten little monsters appear and then disappear from
the page.
ISBN 978-1-59643-627-5
[1. Monsters—Fiction. 2. Counting.] I. Emberley, Ed. II. Title.

PZ7.E5665Te 2012
[E]—dc22
                                                              2010028118

Roaring Brook Press books are available for special promotions and premiums.
For details contact: Director of Special Markets, Holtzbrinck Publishers.

First edition 2011
Printed in April 2011 in China by South China Printing Co. Ltd.,
Dongguan City, Guangdong Province

1 3 5 7 9 8 6 4 2

one little

two little

three little
beasties,

four little

five little

six little

seven little

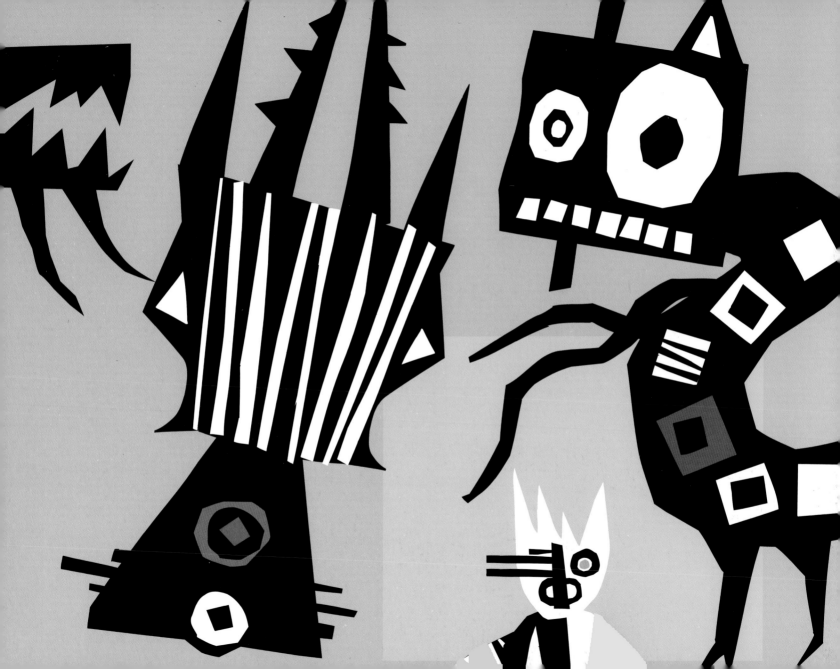

eight little

nine little beasties,

ten little
beasties
dancing.

ten little

nine little

eight little

beasties,

Seven little

six little

five little beasties,

four little

three little

two
little
beasties,

one little beastie dancing.